10 Minute Tales

I0256360

Fireman Sam™

The Great Fire of Pontypandy

When you see these symbols:

Read aloud
Read aloud to
your child.

Read alone
Support your child
as they read alone.

Read along
Read along with
your child.

EGMONT
We bring stories to life

Read aloud   Read along

It was a special day in Pontypandy.

Chief Fire Officer Boyce had come all the way from Newtown to give Fireman Sam a medal for bravery. "Well done, Sam!" he said.

"Thank you, sir!" replied Sam.

Station Officer Steele and the rest of the fire crew were very proud of Sam. He was a hero!

Fireman Sam is getting a medal.
He is a brave hero.

Read aloud   Read along

After the ceremony, Chief Fire Officer Boyce asked Sam to be the Station Officer in Newtown.

Sam knew that being a Station Officer was a very important job. But he wasn't sure that he wanted to move away from Pontypandy.

"I need time to think about the job," Sam told Officer Boyce.

Read alone

Boyce asks Sam to take a job in Newtown.
Sam needs time to think about it.

Read aloud   **Read along**

Later, Sam, Elvis and Radar went to the forest. They put up signs to remind people not to light campfires.

With the weather so hot and dry, a forest fire could spread quickly. Pontypandy would be in great danger!

Before Sam returned to the Fire Station, Elvis asked him, "I'd like to be a hero too. How do you do it?"

"I'm not sure, Elvis," Sam replied with surprise. "I just try to be the best firefighter I can be."

Elvis puts up signs that say not to light fires.
He tells Sam that he wants to be a hero too.

Read aloud   Read along

On the other side of the forest, Trevor helped the children pitch their tents. He had brought them on a camping trip so they could earn their Pontypandy Pioneers survival badge.

Their next task was to gather food from the forest for lunch, but all they could find were a few blackberries. The Pioneers were hungry!

Trevor tried to lead a singsong, but the children were too grumpy to sing. Earning the survival badge was hard work!

The children are on a camping trip.
They get very hungry.

Read alone

Read aloud   Read along

Norman and his cousin Derek had secretly brought some sausages on the trip. They sneaked away to find a place to cook them.

"But there are no fires allowed," Derek said.

"We can't eat raw sausages, can we!" Norman replied as he rubbed two sticks together.

"Norman!" It was his mum, Dilys! The boys left the sticks and ran back to the camp. Suddenly, the sticks burst into flames!

Read alone

Norman and Derek sneak off to cook lunch.
But when they are called back, a fire starts!

Read aloud   **Read along**

At the Mountain Rescue Station,
Tom Thomas looked out of the window.
He spotted a strange cloud over the woods
and looked closer.

It wasn't a cloud, it was smoke from a fire!
Tom called the Fire Station straight away.

"Tom here. I see smoke in the forest,"
he reported to Station Officer Steele.
"I'll try to put out the fire before it
spreads!"

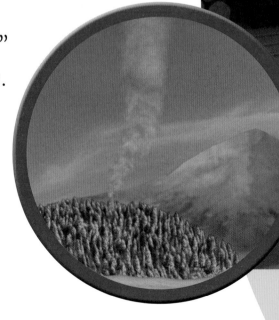

Read alone

Tom sees smoke in the forest.
He tells Officer Steele about the fire.

Read aloud   Read along

With Sam gone, Elvis put up the last of the signs. Suddenly, Elvis' walkie-talkie crackled.

"Cridlington!" shouted Station Officer Steele. "A forest fire has started and there are people on the camp site. You must get them out of danger!"

"You can count on me, sir!" Elvis said. "Let's go, Radar!"

Officer Steele tells Elvis about the forest fire.
Elvis must find the campers.

Read alone

Read aloud   Read along

Tom flew Wallaby One over the forest
and dropped an enormous bucket of water
on to the flames.

"Tom," Sam said over the walkie-talkie. "How
does it look?"

"Not good, Sam," answered Tom. "The wind is
blowing the fire towards Pontypandy!"

"We'll be right there to tackle it from the ground,"
promised Sam.

Read alone

Tom flies to the forest.
He drops water on the fire.

Read aloud   Read along

With lights flashing and sirens wailing, Jupiter and Venus sped to the forest.

Sam, Penny and Station Officer Steele sprayed water on the trees and grass. They hoped that it would stop the flames.

If the fire spread, Pontypandy could be destroyed. It was up to Sam and the crew to save the town!

"Steady now!" called Sam. Fighting this fire would take a lot of teamwork!

Read alone

Sam and the fire crew rush to the forest.
They spray water on the trees and grass.

Read aloud   Read along

Meanwhile, Elvis asked Radar to sniff around the forest. With his clever nose, Radar soon led Elvis right to the campers!

Elvis was happy to find everyone safe, but the thick smoke was making it hard to breathe.

"Follow me!" said Elvis. He heard Jupiter's siren and led the group towards the sound. Finally, they found their way out of the smoky woods.

"Well done, Elvis!" said Sam.

Elvis and Radar find the campers.
Elvis leads them out of the forest

Read aloud **Read along**

Elvis joined the fire crew battling the blaze, but it was too strong for the water hoses.

CRACK! Suddenly, a burning branch broke off from a tree and fell straight towards Sam!

Without thinking, Elvis knocked right into Sam and rolled him to safety. The branch landed on the spot where Sam had been standing.

"Thanks, Elvis!" cried Sam. "You saved my life!"

Read alone

A burning branch falls towards Sam.
Elvis knocks Sam out of the way.

Read aloud   Read along

Despite the crew's hard work, the fire was still heading straight for Pontypandy.

"We must get everyone to safety!" called Station Officer Steele.

The fire crew took the townspeople and their pets to the harbour and helped them on board Charlie's fishing boat. As they watched the fire creep towards Pontypandy, Sarah asked, "Why are we going out into the water, Dad?"

"It's the only place where the fire can't reach us," said Charlie.

Read alone

The fire heads towards the town.
The people get in a boat to be safe.

Read aloud   Read along

As the fire got closer, Sam felt very sad. He didn't want to see Pontypandy destroyed.

Just then, a drop of water fell on his nose. Sam looked up at the clouds. "It's raining!" he shouted.

"Let's hope it's enough to put out the fire!" said Penny as the rain began to pour down.

Tom soon radioed from his helicopter. "The rain has put out the fire. We're out of danger!"

The townspeople cheered as the boat returned to the dock. Pontypandy was safe!

Read alone

It starts to rain very hard.
The rain puts out the fire!

Read aloud   Read along

Soon after, there was another medal ceremony at Pontypandy Fire Station.

"Elvis, you showed real bravery during the Great Fire," Boyce said. "Well done!"

Elvis saluted. Now he was a hero, too!

"And it's my pleasure to give survival badges to the Pontypandy Pioneers," Trevor Evans said next. "Well, to most of them . . ."

"This is all your fault!" Norman and Derek moaned to each other. There were no badges for them!

Elvis gets a medal for being a hero.
The children get badges too!

Read aloud   Read along

Afterwards, Sam told Chief Fire Officer Boyce that he had decided not to take the job in Newtown.

"Why didn't you take it, Sam?" Elvis asked him later. "You could have been a Station Officer in Newtown with your very own crew."

Fireman Sam smiled. "I learned a lot during the Great Fire, Elvis," he said. "I almost lost Pontypandy and now I know I never want to leave. Pontypandy will always be my home!"

Fireman Sam does not take the new job.
Pontypandy will always be his home!

Enjoy more from the
10-Minute Tales range

2010 Practical Pre-School Awards GOLD

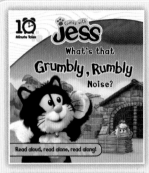

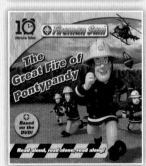

Go online at egmont.co.uk/10minutetales
for puzzles, colouring and activities!

...Ben 10
10-Minute Adventures also available...